The Trolls and Fairy Slipper

THE TROLLS AND FAIRY SLIPPER

© Normannaune
Illustrations: Rolf Lidberg
Original text: Robert Alsterblad
Design: Normannaune
www.normannaune.no
Art.Nr. 3229
ISBN: 82-8057-003-9

The Trolls and Fairy Slipper

Rolf Lidberg

Spring has come and Grandfather Troll is lying in the flowers in the meadow, peering at the things around him. The birds are singing and the sounds of spring can be heard all over Troll Forest. A little way away Thistle the troll boy is sitting making a toy boat from bark.

Grandfather Troll laughs out loud. But then he suddenly remembers a lonely little blue anemone he saw further up the hill.

"Thistle!" he calls. "Shall we go and visit the lonely blue anemone who lives up the hill?"

"Not now, Grandfather," answers Thistle. "I've got to finish my bark boat in time for the competition this afternoon. Let's go and visit her tomorrow."

The next day Grandfather Troll and Thistle pay a visit to the blue anemone. "I feel sorry for her," says Thistle. "Why aren't there any other blue anemones here? After all, flowers are just like trolls - they need friends to be happy."

Grandfather Troll nods in agreement.

"I think Mother Nature will make sure that some other anemones come to live here, perhaps next spring," he comforts Thistle. "Do you remember when we climbed those high cliffs on the other side of the river last year?"

"You mean when we climbed right to the top of the mountain and threw stones into the big lake, and they made ripples all the way to the other side of the lake?"

"Yes, that's right. On the way up Heather saw a little violet all alone on a rock ledge. Do you remember?"

"Was it that dainty little mauve flower?"

"That's the one," answers Grandfather Troll. "Well, I thought that perhaps you and I and Heather could go and see whether she has made any new friends this year. Would you like that?"

Grandfather Troll, Thistle and Heather climb eagerly up the steep cliffs.
"Look how many flowers there are here!" says Heather.
"Yes, Miss Violet has plenty of new friends now," answers Grandfather Troll.
"Mother Nature is very clever," whispers Thistle. "Shall we go right up to the top and throw stones into the lake?"

Later in the summer Father Troll is sitting in the green grass with two talkative troll nymphs.

"Do you know what we saw the other day when we were flying around in Troll Forest?" asks one of the troll nymphs.

"A flower ...," says the other.

"... who was all by herself ...," continues the first troll nymph.

"... and feeling very sad," adds the other.

"And she was scared she might get trodden on ..." says troll nymph number one.

"... by berry pickers," finishes troll number two.

Father Troll almost goes cross-eyed trying to listen to both troll nymphs at once.

"Is that so?" is all he can say.

"The flower's name is Fairy Slipper. And she would very much like to move somewhere else where there are lots of other flowers to keep her company," says troll number one.

"Please, Father Troll, can't you send some trolls to go and see how she is?" asks troll number two, while he tickles Father Troll's beard.

"Well, yes, indeed ... if she's worried about careless berry pickers, we'd better go and talk to her," answers Father Troll.

And that is why the troll family are in the forest looking for Fairy Slipper. The troll nymphs have told them which way to set out, but since troll nymphs always fly around in circles, darting here and there, it isn't easy for the trolls to find Fairy Slipper.

Heather has brought her friend Blossom with her, and Blossom is the first one to catch sight of the flower.

"Look!" cries Blossom. "Over there! There she is!"

"How do you do, Fairy Slipper. The troll nymphs told us that you need some help," says Heather.

"Oh yes, I do. I´m so glad you have come to visit me," she answers. Fairy Slipper tells them how sad and frightened she has been. Just an hour ago a whole class of schoolchildren went past, and almost trampled on her.

"I´m very sorry to hear it," says Heather. "I promise to tell my big brother Thistle where you live, and he is sure to come and help you. But it´s getting late, and we have to hurry back home to Troll Valley now, or else they will wonder where we´ve got to. Goodbye!"

On their way home they meet Thistle, who has been looking for them in the forest. He is also on his way home, but when he hears Heather and Blossom´s story, he turns back into the forest.

"You two go on home," he says. "Tell Father Troll and Mother Troll not to worry about me. I´ll be home as soon as I have finished helping Fairy Slipper."

"We made a trail of sticks and fir cones to help you find the way," says Heather.

"Thank you, that was very kind and thoughtful," says Thistle gratefully.

But Thistle arrives too late. When he gets there, Fairy Slipper has already been trampled underfoot.

"Help!" she begs in a tiny voice. "Please help me find somewhere safer to live."

Thistle digs Fairy Slipper up very carefully. He makes sure he gets all her roots. Then he puts some warm earth round her and places her gently in his rucksack, where she will be safe.

"Come on," he says. "I´m taking you to Troll Lake. I think we´ll find a nice surprise for you there."

It is a long way to Troll Lake and they do not arrive until the next morning. Thistle rows over the lake to a small cove where magic water lilies grow. They are protected by a beautiful lake maiden, and no one is allowed to go near the lilies without asking her first.

Thistle tells the lake maiden what has happened to Fairy Slipper. He asks her politely if she could give Fairy Slipper a few of the special healing drops of medicine he has heard that the lake maiden makes.

"Of course I shall," answers the lake maiden with a smile. "Since your request is for such a noble, unselfish goal, I will give you a few drops of my magic liquid."

First the lake maiden takes some dewdrops from the water lily leaves. Then she adds a few drops of milk, and mixes it all together in a golden bottle.

"Thank you very much!" says Thistle and rows quickly back across the lake. He gives Fairy Slipper a few drops from the bottle, and then they set off again on foot to find a new place for her to live.

After a few minutes Fairy Slipper feels a lot better, and when they arrive at a meadow full of flowers at the edge of a wood she laughs for joy.

"Just look, Thistle! By the edge of the wood here I can rest in the shade, and still be close to all the other flowers in the meadow. I know I will be happy here. This is where I would like to live."

Thistle plants her and waters her with the last few drops from the golden bottle the lake maiden gave him.

"I´m so tired I need to go home and sleep for a few days now," yawns Thistle. "But I´ll send Father Troll to visit you and check that all is well."

When Thistle gets home, Father Troll is very curious and decides to go and visit Fairy Slipper at once.

"There must have been real troll magic in that medicine," says Father Troll when he sees how strong and healthy Fairy Slipper looks.

But Fairy Slipper is not so sure about that.

"I think that the best medicine is having such good friends as Heather and Blossom, and Thistle of course. Without them I wouldn't be so well and happy."

Fairy Slipper´s new home and her fantastic recovery call for celebration! All the flowers and creatures in the meadow invite the trolls to a party to thank them for being such good friends.

The trolls make themselves into tiny trolls so that they can dance in the meadow without trampling on their flower friends - did you know that all trolls can make themselves tiny or huge? They can even make themselves invisible, but they are not allowed to do so except when Prudence, the oldest troll in Troll Valley, gives them special permission.

There is only one troll in Troll Valley who has the magical trollcraft to teach other trolls how to make themselves invisible. He is a small troll boy called Gorse, but this trollcraft is so secret and mysterious that the trolls in Troll Valley do not like talking about it.

The party lasts for several days, and on the third day Bumble Bee says:
"I have written a tune for Thistle and Fairy Slipper. It is called Fairy Slipper´s Waltz."

And he plays an enchantingly beautiful tune. None of the trolls even think of dancing. They just stand there listening, lost in the sweet music.

The music can soon be heard all over Troll Valley. It spreads like wildfire and echoes through all the mountains and valleys. The plants bloom and turn even greener, and the trolls and animals are happy and all help each other.

After a few weeks of playing and dancing the music dies away. But it can still be heard ever so faintly in the valleys, as if it is just resting, waiting for the next party in Troll Valley.

One evening as Father Troll is sitting making supper, he hears the beautiful tune faintly in the distance. He sits back and listens to the music.
"All this is thanks to my troll boy Thistle," he thinks proudly. "Thistle is a smart young troll. Perhaps Gorse will teach him how to make himself invisible soon." A strange smell of burning and Thistle´s voice make him jump.
"Father, you´re burning the supper! Is it ready yet? I´m SO hungry!"

In August Father Troll and Heather go into the forest to see their old friends and make some new ones. They meet one of Fairy Slipper's cousins.

"Hello, my name is Snow Orchid," she says. "I met two troll nymphs who told me all about the troll children's kindness to Fairy Slipper. It would be so nice if I could have some friends nearby too."

"I'll think about it next year," says Father Troll. "The best time of year to move flowers is in the spring. But I can't promise anything."

Little Heather whispers in Snow Orchid's ear just before they set off home.

"I'm almost sure that Father Troll will help you, because he is so kind and always wants everyone to be happy," she says. "But in any case, Thistle the troll boy is my big brother, and he almost always does what I ask."